Adapted by Isabel Gaines
Illustrated by Mark Marderosian and Fred Marvin

First published by Parragon in 2012
Parragon
Queen Street House
4 Queen Street
Bath BA1 1HE, UK
www.parragon.com

ISBN 978-1-4454-4745-2

Printed in China

Disney

Winnie the Pooh

I Love You, Mama

A little story for little learners

PaRragon

Bath • New York • Singapore • Hong Kong • Cologne • Delhi
Melbourne • Amsterdam • Johannesburg • Auckland • Shenzhen

One day, Tigger and
Roo were out bouncing.

They bounced up to
Christopher Robin.

"Hello!" said Tigger
and Roo.
"Hi!" said
Christopher Robin.

"Tomorrow is
Mother's Day,"
said Christopher Robin.

9

Christopher Robin
had an idea.
"We can have
a surprise party,"
he said.

All the friends got
together. They
planned the party.

The next morning, Roo
remembered something.
He had forgotten to get
Mama a present.

Roo looked for
something to give Mama.
But he only had toys.

Roo heard a knock
at the front door.
He ran out of his room.
It was time
for the party.

Kanga opened the door.
"HAPPY MOTHER'S DAY!"
everyone shouted.

"Thank you!"
Kanga said.

"Sit in your
favourite chair,
Mama!" said Roo.

"Time for presents!"
said Roo.

Eeyore gave Kanga
some droopy flowers.

"Tigger has something,
too," said Roo.

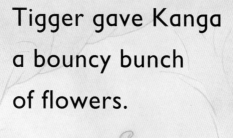

Tigger gave Kanga
a bouncy bunch
of flowers.

"My flowers are not as nice as Tigger's," said Eeyore. "Your flowers are pretty, too," said Kanga.

Christopher Robin

gave out

homemade muffins.

Rabbit gave Kanga
vegetables from
his garden.

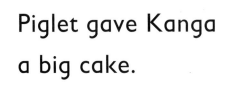

Piglet gave Kanga
a big cake.

Pooh gave
her a pot
of honey.

Owl said a poem.

Kanga clapped.

Owl took a bow.

It was Roo's turn.
But he did not have
a gift for Kanga.
He started to cry.
"I forgot to get you
a present," he said.

"But I already have the best present ever," said Kanga.

"You do?" asked Roo.

"Yes!" said Kanga.

"I have you!"